Ma

in the

Mountains

Madness in the Mountains

Kaye Umansky

illustrated by

Chris Fisher

Hodder
Children's
Books

a division of Hodder Headline

First published in Great Britain in 1999 by
Hodder Children's Books

10 9 8 7 6 4 3 2 1

A Catalogue record for this book is available from the British Library.

ISBN 0340 74375 1

Printed and bound in Great Britain by
Guernsey Press, Guernsey, Channel Islands

Hodder Children's Books
A division of Hodder Headline
338 Euston Road
London NW1 3BH

CONTENTS

For Mo and Ella

THE STORY SO FAR

Neville is having a bad time. His cart is broken and Gran has given away their life savings to a beggar. To make matters worse, they are about to be evicted from their cottage by the old squire unless they can come up with *one hundred gold coins* in backrent! Armed with an axe and Venetia the donkey, Neville sets off to seek his fortune and finds himself in the nearest town. Here, he makes friends with a winsome stray dog, whom he names Spot. Neville finds a lost pocket-book belonging to, Dr Hirasmus Baboom, an alchemist, who claims to have mastered the secret of turning rocks into gold. He rewards Neville with *one hundred gold coins*! Sadly, these turn out to be illegal currency. Thrown into jail, Neville shares a cell with two desperados (Ratsy and Burk the Beserker), members of a fierce mountain bandit tribe, ruled by the very small Big Ma Manky. With the aid of dynamite, Ma Manky springs them all out of jail and offers Neville – or Nev, as he now calls himself – a safe escort home.

Now read on…

CHAPTER 1
TO THE
MOUNTAINS

The world was filled with dust, the thunder of hooves, shouts and the cracking of whips. From somewhere up in front came the sound of shrill, excited barking. Dawn was breaking over the mountains and the sky was streaked with red – not that Nev was able to appreciate much of the view, being currently upside down.

Five riders urged their sweating horses up the steep, winding mountain path. Nev was bringing up the rear. He could hardly be said to be riding. He was tied like a sack of potatoes over Venetia's saddle. Every bone in his body ached. His hair was clogged with dust. All the blood in his body had rushed to his head hours ago and remained there, sloshing around and giving him a blinding headache.

"If this is what they mean by a jail break, they can keep it," he muttered through chapped lips. All things considered, he would sooner have stayed quietly in his cell. Anything was preferable to being

4

almost blown up, dragged out of jail by a mad woman no higher than his knees, forcibly strapped on to his own donkey and dragged up a vertical mountain.

And what a mountain. Up it went. Up, up, up. It never seemed to run out of Up. The path just went on and on. There was a wall of rock rising on one side. On the other – the side over which Nev's head dangled – was a sheer drop, where there was a worrying lot of Down.

Venetia was annoyed at being attached to a leading rein. Determined to show that she was a free spirit, she stepped perilously close to the crumbling edge. Pebbles fell away beneath her hooves.

"Careful!" croaked Nev, from his upside-down position. "Get back, Venetia! We're going ooooverrrrr…"

He shut his eyes and waited for the plunge. It didn't come. When he finally dared to open one eye, Venetia had veered back towards the rock face and the horrible, jolting climb was continuing ever upwards.

The horse in front slowed to allow them to catch up.

"All right, kid?" enquired the rider. He was a short, wiry man with hoops in his ears and a dirty bandana wound around his head. His name was Ratsy. Nev had learned that in the short time they had shared a cell together.

"No," said Nev, staring up into Ratsy's nostrils. "I'm not. I've got a migraine. Let me go."

"Ah, yer all right. Won't be long now."

"Until what? I go over the edge? Let me go."

"Until we reach the hideout. You just hang on in there."

"I can't do much else can I? Lemmegolemmegolemmego."

"Sorry, kid. No can do. Ma's orders."

"Then at least let me ride the right way up," pleaded Nev. "It's horrible like this."

"Nah, you gotta be like that. It's nothin' personal, just the bandit way of doin' things. This is the way we always transports our – er – guests."

"Prisoners, you mean!" cried Nev bitterly.

"Oh, I wouldn't say that."

"I would, then. What I can't understand is, *why?* You won't get any money from my gran, if you're thinking of a ransom. And I'm no good to you for anything else. I can't fight or rob or do any bandity type things. It's just not me."

"Now, now," scolded Ratsy. "That's the old *Neville* talkin'. You're *Nev* now. Where's yer spirit? What about all that talk about bringin' us naughty rogues to justice an' claimin' the reward? You sounded tough enough then."

"That's because I was over-excited," explained Nev. "You get desperate when you need money. I see now I was being a bit over ambitious."

"What's the hold-up, Ratsy?" Another rider had joined them. Nev found himself looking up a new set of miniature nostrils. They belonged to Big Ma Manky, chief of the bandit tribe.

Big Ma certainly did not live up to her name. There were *six-year-olds* taller than Big Ma. Everything about her was pint-sized. Wild grey hair framed her tiny face, which was wrinkled and browner than a walnut. She wore a

tasteful collection of old bits of sack, tied around the middle with string. Her arms were full of wriggling bath mat, which, on closer inspection, turned out to be Nev's dog, Spot.

"No problem, Ma," said Ratsy. "Just givin' the lad a pep talk."

"Bite her, Spot!" cried Nev, desperately. "Go on, boy!"

"Hey, hey!" cried Ma. "That ain't no way ta thank me fer springin' ya outa jail. By the bys, Ratsy here tells me ya come up with a fancy plan to bring us cut-throat banditos to justice an' claim the bounty. How's it goin' so far, d'ya reckon?"

She gave a cackling laugh, exposing an upside-down row of black and gold teeth. Spot stretched out a long, pink tongue and licked her on the nose.

"Oh, Spot," sighed Nev. "How could you?"

"Cute little feller, ain't he?" said Ma, ruffling the shaggy head. "What you call him Spot fer? He ain't got no spot."

"Because I've always wanted a dog called ... oh, never mind," said Nev, wretchedly. "Look, please. Let me go, eh? Just untie me and let me ride away. I promise I won't make trouble."

"Cain't do that, son," said Ma, cheerfully. "What with ya knowin' the way to our secret hide-out an' all. Yer in too deep. Besides, we're short-handed, while Wild Benny's in hospital havin' his teeth removed."

"From someone's leg," explained Ratsy, helpfully.

"But I'm no use to you!" wailed Nev. Venetia shuffled sidewise and his heels scraped painfully on the rock face. "I'm a *woodcutter*. I've been brought up to be – *well, polite*."

"Oh, ya gonna be *useful* all righty," said Ma, dropping a kiss on Spot's head and wheeling her horse around. "I got big plans fer *you*. Now, just you hang on in there quiet, like a good boy, an' we'll be home afore ya knows it. We're takin' the short cut. See ya later. *Yeeeee-ha!*" With that, she dug her heels in the horse's flanks and was off in a cloud of dust – most of which went up Nev's nose.

Ratsy watched him choke for a moment, then gave an encouraging thumbs-up sign and cantered off in her wake, tugging Venetia behind.

It took another agonising ten minutes to reach the top. The ground flattened out and Nev raised his throbbing, dust-caked head and stared through grit-filled eyes, hoping against hope that they had reached their destination. Not so. To his horror, he realised that instead of the land dropping away to his side, it now dropped away in front! Venetia's hooves were inches away from a great ravine, bridged only by a fallen tree. This bounced up and down alarmingly as the bandits, with wild shouts, rode merrily out across the chasm. On the far side, a distant cheer went up and more small figures came rushing out from behind pine trees, whooping and waving their hats. This was evidently the welcoming committee.

"Oh, nooooo…" moaned Nev, as the leading rein tightened and Venetia, with a cross snort, stepped out over the drop. "Please, noooo…"

And then, all around him, was air. He shut his eyes. There was nothing else to do.

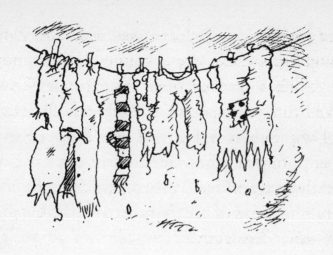

CHAPTER 2
THE HIDE-OUT

Rough hands untied Nev's bonds, pulled him from Venetia's back and set him upright. Immediately, his bloodless legs gave way and he slithered to the ground with a little moan.

"There you go, Nev," said Ratsy's voice. "You can open yer eyes now."

"I can't. They're welded together."

"I'll get you a damp cloth. Hey, Burk! Take

young Nev into the cave and stick 'im in the corner for a while. Get 'is circulation goin'."

Moments later, Nev felt himself being picked up, slung across Burk the Beserker's mighty shoulder and carried for a few feet before being dumped unceremoniously back on the hard floor again. He lay there, groaning feebly as the blood in his head retraced its painful route back down his legs.

All around him, he could hear celebratory cries and back-slapping noises. There was a smell, too. Stew? Or something. Footsteps approached and a nasty-smelling wet cloth dropped onto his face.

"There you go, son," said Ratsy's voice. "Get the trail dust outa yer eyes."

Slowly, painfully, Nev eased himself into a sitting position and went to work with the cloth. After several minutes of gentle dabbing, his left eye sluggishly peeled open, followed shortly by the right. Groggily, he peered around.

He was propped against a rock in the corner of a vast cave. Flickering torches were stuck in niches in the walls. Shadows danced among the stalactites hanging from the roof. A fire crackled merrily in the centre of the floor with a steaming pot set on the top. This was presided over by a small, fierce-looking man with a pencil moustache and a dirty white cook's hat.

The gang were dotted around the place, tucking into bowls of brown, lumpy stuff. Some sat on rocks. Others reclined on straw-filled mattresses draped with ragged pieces of sacking. Big Ma Manky sat in miniature state on what appeared to be the only piece of proper seating – a battered armchair covered in balding red velvet, which looked as though it had spent several winters in a ditch being mauled by mad

bears. Much to Nev's disgust, he saw that Spot was curled up on her lap, eyes fixed hopefully on the bowl she held in her hands.

There was a makeshift washing line, hung with what looked like a scarecrow's cast-offs. Tin mugs hung from hooks that had been hammered into the rock face. Shafts of daylight filtered through a ragged curtain of roughly stitched sacks hanging over the cave mouth.

Ratsy spotted him looking and beckoned him over towards the fire.

"Hey! How's it goin', kid? Come on over an' meet the boys." He gave the rock next to him an encouraging little pat. "Give 'im a bite to eat, Antoine. That'll cheer 'im up."

Nev thought about it. It wouldn't do to appear too friendly and make this gang of ruffians think he approved of their lifestyle. On the other hand, it was cold in the corner. Water was dripping from an overhead stalactite directly onto his feet. Besides, he was starving.

Aching in every limb, he rose stiffly to his

feet, stumbled across the cave, and slumped next to Ratsy. A bowl was thrust in his hands. He looked up to find himself staring into the fierce black eyes of the man in the chef's hat. Antoine, presumably.

"You eet," instructed Antoine.

Immediately, the traitor Spot jumped down from Ma's lap and trotted over to Nev. He sat back on his haunches and dangled his paw in familiar begging pose.

"Just don't talk to me, all right?" snapped Nev.

He stared down into the bowl. Brown lumps of something swam about in a brown pool of something else. He poked at the mess with a spoon.

"What is it?" he enquired. Antoine let loose with a string of incomprehensible words, accompanied by a lot of arm waving.

"He's French," explained Ma Manky. "It's Bandit Stew."

"What's in it?"

"Just eat it and don't ask questions. He takes pride in his work, does Antoine."

Antoine was standing with his arms folded and his eyebrows raised. In one hand, he held a long, sharp butcher's knife. It was clear that he was expecting a positive response.

Nev raised the spoon to his lips and tasted. Hot brown lumps in hot brown sloppy stuff. Disgusting.

"Eees good?" demanded Antoine, fingering the knife.

"Oh, yes," said Nev hastily. "Very – er – brown. Yum yum"

"That's the spirit," said Ratsy, clapping

him on the back. "All friends together, eh? Now then. I'll do the honours, shall I? You've met Ma already. An' you know Burk, o' course."

"URURURURUR…"

Ma Manky reached out and smacked the huge Berserker on his meaty forearm.

"You can quit that right off, Burk," she said sharply. "No berserkin' in the cave. Ya knows the rules."

"Urur," muttered the man mountain, and obediently subsided.

"An' now you know Antoine," continued Ratsy. "And that there's Willy the Kid." A wizened little man sitting cross-legged in a corner looked up and grinned through toothless gums.

"Fastest knife in the North," he announced proudly, reaching behind his shoulder. There was a blur, a flash of silver and something sharp whizzed past Nev's ear and pinged on the rock behind him. "See?"

"And that there's Friendly Fernando," continued Ratsy, pointing at a surly ruffian in a sombrero and poncho, sitting a little apart from the rest.

"Get-a lost, gringo," snarled Friendly Fernando, darkly.

"Pay no mind, that's just 'is way," said Ratsy, cheerfully. "E's delightful when you get to know 'im."

"I keel you, Ratsy," growled the delightful one.

"An' this here's No Soap Nigel," continued Ratsy, pointing to a wild-haired man who was currently sucking stew off dirt-encrusted fingers. "I wouldn't get down wind of 'im, if I was you," he added, meaningfully. "Not a great one for washin', are you, No Soap?"

"Brings me out in a rash," agreed No

Soap Nigel. "Shockin' stuff, water. Brrrr." He gave a theatrical little shiver.

"So there you have it," said Ratsy. "That's us. Apart from Wild Benny, who's…"

"…having his teeth removed from someone's leg," Nev finished off for him. "You've already mentioned him, thanks. But if you think I can fill in for him, you're wrong. I'm not biting anyone, and that's final."

"Oh, we ain't expectin' ya to *bite*," said Ma, wiping up the last of her stew with a chunk of bread. "Nope. That ain't what I got in mind for you at all."

"What, then?" said Nev.

"Write," said Ma. "Ratsy here been tellin' me ya can hold a pencil. Ya can write the notes."

"Notes?"

22

"*Ransom* notes! The notes what needs writin' when we kidnaps folks and holds 'em fer ransom. Ain't none of us kin read or write. Up to now, I always had ter send a couple of the boys down into town an' get the scribe to do 'em. An' he charges an arm an' a leg, on account o' the – er – *delicate* contents, if you git my meaning."

"Mmm," said Nev. "Yes. I suppose I do."

"An' when the boys goes down into town, they tends to end up in the Crossed Axes. Which leads ter trouble. An' then I gotta mosey on down maself an' blast 'em out o' jail, and that's a waste of good dynamite." She glared at Ratsy and Burk, who both looked sheepish. "But now we got you, darlin', so no prob-lemo."

"I'm not so sure about that," said Nev, stoutly. "You can't force me to take part in your nasty criminal activities. I might remind you that you *said* you'd give me an escort home."

Ma gave a short laugh. "Yeah. Well, I was lyin'. An' now yer here, ya might as well pitch in. There's plenty o' chores needs doin' around the place. We'll keep ya busy, don't fret. Then, if ya shows willin', we'll try ya on a proper job. But ya can start by doin' the washin' up. There's a stream a few hundred yards up the track. Give him a bucket, Ratsy. Willy, you go with him. Mind he don't scarper."

"Come on, son," said Willy the Kid. "Don't look so glum. It ain't a bad life, you'll see."

"Mmm," sighed Nev. Reluctantly, he picked up the bucket. As far as he could see, it was a very bad life indeed.

CHAPTER 3
THE HOLD-UP

"So this is what bandits do, is it?" said Nev. "Sit around in prickly bushes all day, waiting for business."

"Most o' the time," agreed Willy the Kid.

The two of them were sitting in a clump of prickly bushes, watching the trail that wound away below them. It was a different trail to the short cut that they had taken three days earlier. It was wider, with wheel ruts baked into the hard dirt. Apparently, it was the main road over the mountain.

A short way below them, No Soap Nigel was crouching behind a rock. You couldn't see him – but then again, you didn't have to. No Soap always made his presence smelt. Friendly Fernando was perched in a tree overhead, acting as Look Out. You couldn't see him either, but every so often you could hear him spitting. Nev shuddered. The gang really did have most unsavoury habits.

He sighed and moved his cramped legs. This was his first proper job. Despite himself, he had been looking forward to it. Anything was better than the thousand and one ghastly jobs there were to do when living in a cave.

For the past three days Nev had fetched water, chopped kindling, tended the fire, peeled potatoes, swept the floor, washed stew bowls, held Ma's knitting wool, cleaned and polished weapons, attached nosebags to wild-eyed horses and boiled kettles for the countless mugs of tea the bandits consumed. In the evenings, when the mugs of tea were replaced by countless jugs of whisky, he would be expected to join in the

choruses of rowdy bandit songs, accompanied by the wheezing strains of Willy the Kid's mouth organ. This would be followed by an hour or so of watching the bandits shoot at bottles. Only after he had swept up the broken glass would he be allowed to flop onto his straw mattress and fall into an exhausted sleep – only to be roughly roused at the crack of dawn, when the whole grim business would start all over again.

Each day, Big Ma would send out two or three of the bandits to watch the trail in the hopes that some unsuspecting traveller might come by. So far, none had, and they would return in the evening sadly shaking their heads and demanding supper, which was always

Bandit Stew. Ma herself never went on these expeditions. She preferred to stay in the cave, snoozing or clipping her toenails in the tiny hammock erected in one of the few dry parts of the cave.

Sometimes she sat in her huge armchair with a wooden box on her lap, counting and re-counting her ill-gotten gains. Judging from her heavy sighs, Nev had the feeling that times were hard. Sometimes, if the sun was shining, she sat on a rock in the entrance, knitting woolly hats for the boys or smoking a tiny clay pipe or feeding biscuits to Spot. Traitor Spot.

Nev was usually left in the tender care of Antoine the cook – a hard taskmaster.

Helping Antoine was no picnic. Apart from anything else, Nev couldn't understand a single word he said. A one-way communication was established between them, which consisted of Antoine hitting Nev over the head with a spoon.

Now, though, Nev was out on his first job. Ratsy and Burk were out hunting for small fluffy things to put in the Bandit Stew and Ma had decided that he, Nev, should go on Trail-Watching Duty to make up the numbers. Granted, it was nice to be out of the way of Antoine's spoon for once, but Trail-Watching was not the sort of occupation people would queue up for. It was mindlessly, tediously boring. After three hours of it, he found himself quite looking forward to the times when Friendly Fernando would spit. He found he was making little bets with himself as to when it would happen.

Now, he would think. *Any minute now. I'll just count to three, and he'll do it. One, two...*

Hrrrrkkk! Splat! And Nev would feel quite pleased with himself.

He was quite relieved when Willy the Kid crawled into the clump of prickle bushes to join him.

"The trail isn't used much, I take it?" said Nev, nodding at the empty road.

"Nope," said Willy. "Folks with any sense avoids these mountains like the plague 'cos they knows they'll get robbed by us."

"So what's the point?"

"Well…" Willy scratched his whiskers and thought about this. "Well, yer best hope is a luckless stranger. Some nobleman or rich merchant who ain't heard of our fearsome reputation. But that don't happen often. Sometimes ya git the odd shepherd boy. We jumped one the other week, pinched his sandwiches. Lovely, they was. Cheese an' pickle."

"And that's *it*? Hours of waiting in prickly bushes on a cold mountainside for a *cheese sandwich?*"

"And pickle," Willy reminded him.

"Still," said Nev. They sat in silence for a

while. After a bit, Nev said:

"So why do they call you the Kid, Willy?"

"Why not?" said Willy.

"Well – doesn't it perhaps strike you that you're, well, not to put too fine a point on it, a little, shall we say, erm – old?"

"So?" Willy sounded rather snappish. "Big Ma ain't big. Your dog Spot ain't got a spot. I can call myself whatever I darn-tootin' well likes. An' if yer gonna make personal remarks, young Nev, I reckon I'll go an' join No Soap over behind that rock…"

He broke off. A soft whistle came from overhead. Fernando's face peered from between the branches. He was making frantic signals.

"Hold it!" said Willy, excitedly. "Hold yer horses, my son. I gotta a feelin' this might just be our lucky day!"

Cautiously, he stuck his head above the prickle bush and signalled for Nev to do the same. Nev bobbed his head up and looked at where Willy's finger pointed. Far below, there was a cloud of dust advancing up the trail.

"It's a coach!" whooped Willy, clutching his stomach with excitement. "A rootin' tootin' *coach*! Now you'll see some action, boy, an' no messin'."

Nev's mouth went dry. He wasn't sure he wanted to see some action. It would make a change from boredom, to be sure – but boredom was safe. Action was – well, possibly rather scary.

"Git *down*!" hissed Willy. "D'ya want 'em ter *see* ya? You stay right there, an' don't move 'til I tells yer."

Nev ducked down. Willy was crouched beside him, a gleaming knife now held in each hand. They could hear the sound of the coach wheels and horses' hooves. Behind them, there was a light thud as Friendly Fernando dropped to the ground and joined them in the prickle bushes. A slim dagger was gripped between his teeth.

"Look," said Nev. "Look, I hope nobody's about to be hurt. I don't believe in violence. Gran always says…"

"Shut up-a your face, gringo," hissed Fernando, producing a large blunderbuss from beneath his poncho. Nev swallowed and shut up his face. The sound of the approaching coach was getting louder. Sweat poured down Nev's brow. His stomach churned. He could hear the creak of the wheels and crack of the whip as the driver urged the horse up the steep slope. Then...

BANG! There came the sound of a gunshot. Nev whimpered and covered his eyes. Seconds later, when he dared uncover them, he found that he was alone. From somewhere nearby came the mixed sounds of shouting, neighing and a thin, high-pitched screaming. Dreading what he might see, he got into a half-crouch and peered over the tops of the prickle bushes.

The coach had come to a halt a short way down the trail. It was a smart two-seater, with a crest on the door. The coachman was attempting to calm the startled horse whilst keeping his hands in the air. No Soap, Willy and Fernando were milling around, barking orders and doing a lot of menacing weapon-waving.

"Don't shoot!" quavered the coachman – a grizzled old man in a slouch hat. "I gotta bad back!"

"Belt up, grandad, and get that there horse

under control!" ordered No Soap Nigel.

"I'm tryin', I'm tryin'!"

Friendly Fernando strode to the door. The screams intensified as he wrenched it open. "Out," he ordered. "Step-a down, or eet be the worse for you, my friends!"

"An' stop that there hollerin'," added Willy. "It's doin' my head in."

"That goes for me, too," said a clear voice from inside the coach. "Get a grip, nanny, do."

The screaming dwindled away, to be replaced by noisy sobbing.

"Tell 'er ter stop that blubbin' an' all," said Willy.

"You heard the gentleman, nanny. He wants you to stop crying. Here. You can borrow my handkerchief."

"Oh, but Miss Marietta, them's brigands! Oh boo, hoo, hoo, what shall we do?"

"Get out, of course, as we've been told. I'll go first. Calm down, nobody will hurt you if you do as they say."

"Oh, boo hoo hoo! Oh, miss…"

There was a short pause. Then a small foot appeared on the running board and the first passenger climbed out.

It was a girl. She looked about Nev's age, wearing a blue velvet cloak and a blue bonnet, trimmed with daisies. Two long, brown plaits poked out on either side. In one hand, she carried a blue matching muff. The other held a drawstring bag. She regarded the bandits with an unblinking blue gaze.

"Right," she said, crisply. "What's all this about? Who's the spokesman here?"

No Soap, Willy and Fernando looked at each other uncertainly. Willy cleared his throat.

"That'll be me," he said. "Er – stand and deliver."

"I am standing, if you hadn't noticed."

"The other one ain't, though," pointed out Willy. "You both gotta do it."

"Fair enough. Come along, nanny, you heard him. Out you get."

"Oh noooooo..." wailed the voice inside the coach. "Oooh, Miss Marietta, I'm scared!"

"We're all waiting, nanny dear," said the girl, tapping her foot with a certain amount of exasperation. "The sooner you get out, the sooner we can get all this nonsense sorted."

"Ooooooh..."

The coach rocked as a plump, tear-stained woman in a grey travelling cloak heaved herself down and stood weeping uncontrollably into a hanky.

"Right, gentlemen," continued the girl. "As you can see, we're both standing. Now, exactly what do you require us to deliver?"

"That," said Willy, pointing to the large

37

trunk that was strapped to the roof of the coach. "Fer a start."

A wail went up from Miss Marietta's tear-sodden companion.

"Ooooh! Miss Marietta! Not all yer pretty frocks, what I spent all night up ironin'…"

"Do shut up, nanny, there's a dear," said the girl. Her nanny blew her nose, hiccoughed, and subsided into low-level grizzling.

"You," said No Soap, gesturing to the coachman, who was hunched in his seat, trying to look inconspicuous. "Get the trunk down, and quick about it."

"It's rather heavy," said the girl. "I'm not sure Mr McBucket can manage it. With his bad back."

"She's right there," agreed the coachman. "I can't."

"Go on, No Soap," said Willy. "Get it down."

"No way," said No Soap. "I'm keepin' em covered with me gun. Fernando can do it."

"Get-a lost, steenky," growled Friendly

Fernando. "Theenk I'm a porter?"

"Where's young Nev got to?" said Willy, looking round.

"Er – here," said Nev. With a sinking heart, he stepped out of the prickle bushes.

"What ya doin' over there?" cried Willy. "Doncha know there's a robbery goin' on?"

"You said I had to stay put until you told me to move," objected Nev. "That's what you said."

"Well, now I'm-a tellin' ya ter git up there an bring that trunk down. Hurry it up, we ain't got all day."

"All right, all right!" Nev looked over and met the girl's unflinching blue eyes. "I'm awfully sorry about this," he added. The girl gave a shrug.

Feeling rotten, he stepped onto the running board, reached up and began to tug at the ropes that secured the trunk. Down below, the robbery proceeded.

"We'll have that there sparkly bracelet you're wearin', miss," said Willy. Fernando

removed his sombrero and held it out.

"Oh, no!" moaned the nanny. "Not her priceless, genuine sapphire bracelet!"

Ignoring her, Marietta calmly removed the bracelet and threw it into the hat.

"An' them pretty rings," added Willy.

"Oh nooooo! Not her valuable antique diamond rings what 'ave been 'anded down through countless generations..."

"Nanny," said Marietta, sweetly, taking off the rings and dropping them into the hat. "If you don't shut up, I will ring your neck."

"But they was a goin' away present! That's what you said! His lordship'll be that mad..."

"Goin' away somewhere, are we, miss?"

enquired Willy, conversationally. "Bit of a holiday? Nice weather fer it."

"Actually, it's not a holiday, Mr – er?"

"Kid. Willy the Kid."

"Mr the Kid. I'm off to Dame Hortensia Bonnet's Academy for Young Ladies. It's a finishing school, if you really want to know."

"Is that right? An' what do they learn yer at a place like that? We'll 'ave the purse too, miss, if you don't mind."

"Dull stuff. Embroidery. Flower arranging. Croquet. That sort of thing." She

dropped the purse into the sombrero.

"That's her precious tuck money, you wicked men!" wailed nanny. Everyone ignored her.

"Sounds nice, finishin' school," chipped in No Soap, with a touch of envy. "I've always fancied that there embroidery. Do they make you wash, though?"

"Frequently," nodded Marietta, with a little smile. "Behind the ears, too."

"Brrrrrr," shivered No Soap, going pale behind his layer of grime.

"I expect yer daddy's got a load o' dosh?" enquired Willy. "Must have. Sendin' ya off ter a fancy place like that."

"He's not her daddy. He's her uncle. And he happens to be a Courgette," announced nanny, with a sudden flash of spirit.

"Oh yeah? An' my aunty's a lettuce," put in No Soap, to general amusement. Nanny drew herself up.

"I am referring," she said, "to Lord Courgette, of Courgette Towers. A very important man hereabouts. In fact, he's the richest man in the kingdom, *including* the king. When he hears about this, he'll..."

"That'll do, nanny," interrupted Marietta. "I'm sure no one wants to hear about Uncle."

"Oh, but we do," said Willy. "That's just where you're wrong, miss. We wanna hear all about 'im. Like, fer instance, how much he might be persuaded to cough up to get his lovely little niece back safe and sound. What d'ya reckon?"

Nanny went pale.

"You wouldn't dare!" she gasped. "That's kidnapping! You wouldn't dare!"

"Wouldn't we just?" beamed Willy. "Especially now we got young Nev here to write the ransom note. That makes it all so much simpler. How ya doin' with that trunk, Nev?"

"All right," said Nev, undoing the last rope and heaving away. The trunk slid onto his shoulders. It was a lot heavier that it looked. His knees buckled under the weight and he toppled backwards with a little cry. Both he and the trunk landed on the ground at Marietta's feet.

The trunk burst open, depositing its frilly contents over his head.

"Ooh," said No Soap Nigel, casting his eyes over the piles of silken gowns. "Pretty."

"Get up, Nev," ordered Willy, crossly. "What you think yer playin' at? Pick 'em up this minute. He's new," he explained to Marietta. "We just got him to write the notes."

Red in the face, Nev picked himself up and began to stuff the dresses back into the trunk, helped by No Soap Nigel, who kept holding them up against himself, displaying an unexpected appreciation of beautiful things.

"Yes," said Marietta. "Well, this is all very interesting, but what happens next?"

"Ah. Right," said Willy. "Well, I'll run yer through the procedure. You comes back along of us to the cave, right? And *you*…" – he pointed at the coachman – "can turn around and take *her*…" – he pointed to nanny – "right back where she came from."

"Right away, sir, right away," agreed the coachman, hastily picking up the reins. "Get in, Mrs Wilikins, let's get out of here."

"Noooo!" wailed nanny, bursting into fresh sobs. "You're not taking my baby! My little angel! Not my precious little Marietta, what I dangled on me knee…"

"Just go home, nanny, would you?" said Marietta, wearily. "I'll be quite all right. It can't be any worse than finishing school."

"And you can tell yer uncle don't call us, we'll call him," added Willy. "A ransom note will arrive in due course. When we've decided how much to do him for."

"Get *in*, Mrs Wilikins" urged the coachman, who had lost no time in getting the coach turned around. "Or shall I leave you be'ind?"

Hastily, nanny climbed in. The coachman flicked his whip and the coach moved off at a brisk clip. The last they saw of nanny was a swollen face pressed against the window, mouth opened in an 'O'.

"Right," said Marietta briskly, as the dust cloud receded down the trail. "That's got rid of her." To everyone's surprise, she removed her bonnet and threw it into the branches of a nearby tree. Then she hurled her velvet muff into the prickle bushes, kicked off both of her shoes and looked around with a bright smile. "That's better. Now then. Let's go and see this cave of yours, shall we? It's this way, I take it?"

And without a backward glance she strode

off up the trail. Willy, Fernando and No Soap exchanged startled glances, then hastened off after her, leaving Nev behind to struggle with the trunk.

Briefly, he wondered whether to make a break for it. Now was as good a time as any. But then again, it would mean leaving Spot and Venetia behind, not to mention his axe and his spare socks. Besides, things were getting rather interesting.

CHAPTER 4
MARIETTA

"Ma! We've hit the jackpot!" yelled Willy, running into the cave. "We've got a Courgette!"

Antoine looked up hopefully from his cooking pot. Edible greens were hard to come by. A courgette would make a nice change from dandelion leaves. Burk and Ratsy were sitting in a corner, polishing their hunting knives.

"A what?" said Ratsy.

"URUR?" enquired Burk.

"Eh?" said Ma, peering over her knitting. "What you on about, Willy?"

Willy stood proudly to one side.

"In you come, miss," he said. "Meet Big Ma Manky, our leader."

"How do you do?" said Marietta, advancing into the cave and dropping a little curtsy. "I'm very pleased to meet you, Mrs Manky. I'm Marietta Courgette. May I be the first to congratulate you and the boys on a successful kidnapping." Burk's mouth dropped open at this unexpected apparition. Ratsy reached across with a dirty finger and pushed it shut.

"You see?" crowed Willy. "She got nice manners, ain't she? That's on account of her uncle bein' a lord. Regular moneybags, by all accounts."

"Hmm," said Ma. "That right?" She set aside her knitting and climbed down off her armchair. She walked up to Marietta and peered up at her sternly. "Well, miss, I hope you won't be expectin' nothin' fancy. We lives plain up here. You'll have to put up with our rough 'n' ready ways."

"Oh, don't worry about me," said Marietta, breezily. She stared around interestedly at the squalid, smoke-filled, dripping interior. "What a lovely cave! You've made it so cosy, with the fire and everything. All those dinky little hooks for your mugs. And such an effective use of sacking."

"Well, I dunnos 'bout that..." began Ma, rather flustered at receiving such a stream of compliments.

"No, really! I love it! And, oh, what a sweet little dog!" Marietta pounced delightedly on Spot, who wagged his stumpy tail and nuzzled hopefully in her pockets.

"That's young Nev's dog," Ratsy told her.

"By the way – where is young Nev?"

"Here," panted Nev, staggering in with the trunk. He set it down with a crash, then straightened, clutching at his back. "Whoo! That was a killer!"

"Thank you so much," said Marietta. "That was very kind of you. Although, of course, I shan't be needing most of it, now I'm living in a cave. What's your dog's name?"

"Spot. And don't tell me he hasn't got any. I know."

Crossly, Nev flung himself onto his mattress. He felt rather annoyed that nobody had given him credit for not running away when he had the chance. Nobody seemed to care that he had put his back out, either. Sulkily, he reached beneath his straw-filled pillow and brought out a hunk of stale bread he had saved from breakfast. Spot immediately trotted over and laid his head on his knees.

"What you doin' lyin' down, Nev?" demanded Ma. "We got ourselves a visitor. Place is a tip. Get them bowls washed out. The little lady'll be hungry. Hop to it!"

Wearily, Nev hopped to it…

———————————

There was no doubt about it. Marietta Courgette was a big hit with the bandits. Considering her background, she was surprisingly lacking in snobbery. That first night, she tucked into Antoine's stew, declared it delicious and asked for seconds. She willingly joined in with the rowdy singing and complimented Willy on his mouth organ playing. She told Burk he was a big, strong fellow and made him blush. She accepted Ratsy and No Soap's invitation to join them in a game of cards and beat them hollow, winning back her bracelet and

all her rings. She politely declined to sip from the whisky jar, but made up for it by drinking enough mugs of strong tea to sink a battleship. Even Friendly Fernando appeared to be won over, and spent quite a long time fixing up a special hammock and sacking curtain for her in a relatively draught-free corner.

As Nev drifted off that night, exhausted from all his chores, it was to the sound of Marietta merrily taking pot shots at the row of bottles the bandits had set up on a rock.

"Very good, Señorita," Friendly Fernando

was saying. "But squeeze the treeger gently, like thees – look, I show you…"

When Nev awoke the following morning, Marietta was already up and deep in conversation with Ma. They were toasting their toes before the fire and sipping companionably from large mugs of tea.

"The trouble is, ya see, darlin', there ain't no point in gettin' in nice stuff," Ma was saying. "The boys just mucks it all up. That's why I sticks mainly to sackin'. It ain't purty, but it's darn practical."

"You are so right," agreed Marietta. "In your place, it would have been my first choice too. It keeps out the draughts and doesn't show the dirt."

"True. 'Course, in my heart of hearts, I'd just love some o' them lace curtains."

"Well, yes. Lace *is* rather pretty. But it takes a lot of looking after."

"Exactly. The boys'd ruin it in no time. I tell you, ain't no point. I've given up on fancy furnishin's an' fittin's. I got ma old armchair, an' that'll do me. 'Course it's had it's day really."

"Oh, I don't know. We could always smarten it up with a few scatter cushions. We could cut up one or two of my dresses."

"Oh, we couldn't do *that*..."

"Of course we could. What use are they to me? I've got a pink satin one that might do... oh, good morning, Nev. The kettle's on. Shall I make you some tea?"

"People don't make tea fer Nev," said Ma. "Nev makes tea fer people. It's one of his jobs."

"Where is everyone?" asked Nev, yawning and staring around. Even Antoine had deserted his post at the cooking pot. He noticed that someone had swept up the broken glass. All the mattresses were straight, and things seemed generally more – well, orderly.

"Gone fer a wash in the stream," said Ma.

"A *wash*?" Nev couldn't believe his ears. At no time in the past four days had the bandits ever shown signs of wanting a wash. "What – even No Soap?"

"He was the first off."

"Where's Spot?"

"They've taken him too. Gonna give him a bath, they said. Look, git yerself some tea and clear off out of it, will ya? Cain't ya see we're tryin' ter have us a girly conversation here?"

Outside, it was cool, but sunny. Venetia, grazing under the trees with the other horses, looked up and gave a hopeful honk. Nev automatically patted his pocket for a carrot. There wasn't one, of course. Venetia snorted and turned her back.

There came a jolly bark and Spot came skittering down the slope, soaking wet and looking slightly bewildered.

"Hey, Spot!" called Nev. "Here, boy! My, you're wet!"

Spot came rushing up, stopped short, shook himself violently all over Nev, then rushed past him into the cave, where Ma and Marietta were breaking open a packet of biscuits.

"What *is* it with my animals?" muttered Nev.

He heard the sound of voices. Willy, Ratsy, Burk, Fernando, Antoine and No Soap came marching down the track with skins pinkly gleaming and hair plastered to their heads.

Nev hardly recognised them. Burk was holding a bunch of wild flowers in his hand.

"Mornin', Nev," said Ratsy. "Lovely day for a wash."

"Oh yes?" said Nev. "Why today, in particular?"

"Oh, no reason. Well, I don't know about you boys, but I'm ready for some clean socks."

"*Clean socks?*"

"I don't 'ave any clean socks," fretted No Soap Nigel. "Can I borrow yours, Nev?"

"No," said Nev, shortly. There was no way he was going to give up his spare socks. Apart from his axe, they were all he had to remind him of home.

"Oh, leave 'im," said Ratsy. "He's in a moody. Let's go an' 'ave a shave before Miss Mar – I mean, before breakfast."

"You're too late," Nev told him, with a smirk. "She's already up."

Rather sheepishly, the bandits filed past him into the cave.

Nev sat on a rock and sipped his tea. He wondered what Gran was doing now. Perhaps she was sitting at the cottage window, waiting for him to come up the path, joyfully waving a bag of gold coins and shouting that all their troubles were over. He sighed deeply. Time was going by and he was no nearer to his goal. In fact, his situation was worse than ever. He had to do something – and soon.

Before long, a familiar smell came wafting out.

"Breakfast is ready," said Marietta, sticking her head out. In one hand, she held a bowl of stew. "Don't you want some?"

"No thanks," said Nev. He gave a little sigh. "I don't feel all that hungry."

"I'll have it then," said Marietta. "This mountain air makes me ravenous. Mind if I join you?"

She came out and sat companionably next to him. Nev watched her tucking into the vile slop. She really seemed to enjoy it. He thought about Gran's dainty little cucumber sandwiches and sighed again.

"Penny for your thoughts," said Marietta.

"I was thinking about home," said Nev, wistfully. "Wishing I was there right now."

"Really?" said Marietta. "That's the last place I want to be. Apart from Dame Hortensia Bonnet's Academy for Young Ladies, of course." She gave him an odd little smile. "I suppose you think that's strange?"

"Well, yes. I do, actually."

"That's because you haven't met Uncle.

59

But I don't want to talk about him. Tell me about you. You're not a real bandit, are you?"

"No," said Nev. "I'm just a woodcutter. I'm supposed to be seeking my fortune, but it hasn't worked out too well so far. I got mixed up with this lot by accident."

"Really? How?"

"Oh, it's a long story. You wouldn't be interested."

"Oh, but I am! Do tell."

And before he knew it, Nev was telling her about the series of unlikely events that had happened since he left home five – or was it six? – long days ago. She was a good listener. She gasped and tutted sympathetically and widened her blue eyes in all the right places.

" ...that's the way of it," Nev finished. "I have three more weeks to get the hundred gold coins, or we lose the cottage. So I'm just waiting for a chance to make my escape. When I do, I'll take you with me, of course," he added nobly.

"Oh, that won't be necessary," said Marietta. "It's very kind of you, but I'm quite capable of looking after myself. I'll help *you*,

though, if you like."

"How?"

"Well, it needs a bit of careful planning. I'll need to think about it for a bit, but I'm sure we can come up with something…"

"Nev! You're wanted!" Willy was beckoning to him from the cave. "Ma says ya gotta write the ransom note."

"Oh, goody!" said Marietta, jumping up clapping her hands. "What fun!" And she ran into the cave. Nev stared after her. What a peculiar girl. Shaking his head, he shuffled in after her.

Inside, an orange crate had been set out

with a pencil and piece of paper all ready and waiting.

"Time ya earned yer keep, son," said Ma. "Sooner we get the business done, the sooner Marietta can go home."

"Oh, don't worry about me," said Marietta, brightly. "I *like* it here."

"Hmm. Well, even so, we need to get things sorted. Now then. How much shall we demand? That's the question."

"If you want my advice, don't stint yourselves," advised Marietta. "Uncle's *terribly* rich, you know."

"What, then? Shall we say – one hundred gold coins?"

"Oh, much more than that," said Marietta, firmly. "A hundred would go nowhere, split between you. If I were you, I'd go for a hundred each."

The bandits looked quite taken aback. They had taken many hostages in their time, but never one who seemed keen to push her own ransom up.

"Whooo!" said Ma. "Seven hun'red gold coins. That's an awful lot, darlin'."

"Eight," said Marietta. "You're forgetting Nev."

"He's new," Ma explained. "He ain't done no banditin' ta speak of."

"Besides," said Ratsy, "Nev's an *honest* lad, ain't yer, boy? You wouldn't feel right about takin' a cut from the proceeds of our nasty criminal activities, would yer?"

"Er…"

"Maybe not," cut in Marietta. "But he can think of it as being paid very highly for doing the washing up, can't you, Nev?" She gave him an encouraging wink.

"Well…"

"That's settled, then," said Marietta, brightly. "A hundred each. It's not as if Uncle can't afford it."

"So what shall I write, then?" asked Nev, picking up the pencil.

Everyone had ideas about what should go in the ransom note, particularly Marietta. Finally, after a lot of argument and scribbling out and people breathing down his neck, Nev slammed down his pencil and announced: "There. That'll do. I'm not doing it again and that's final."

"Read it out, then," said Ma. So he did. This is what it said:

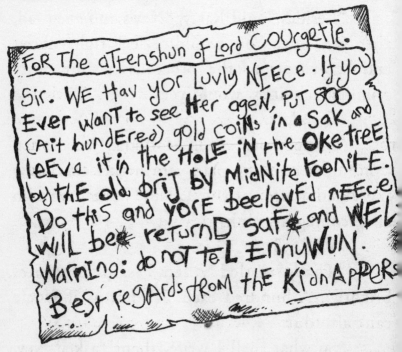

FoR The aTTenshun oF Lord COUrgeTTe.

Sir. WE Hav yor Luvly NEEce. IF you Ever wanT to see Her ageN, PuT 800 (Ait hundEred) gold coiNs in a Sak and leEva it in the HoLE iN the OkE treE by thE old briJ By MidNite toonite. Do this and yore BeeLoved nEEce will bee returnD saFe and WEL Warning: do noT teL EnnyWuN. BEst regArds From the KidnAPPers

"Perfect," said Ma, admiringly. "I think that says it all."

"Now what happens?" asked Marietta, excitedly.

"Well, now we wraps the note round a rock, see. An' a volunteer has ter ride down to yer uncle's place an' chuck it through the winder. Then it's a simple question o' waitin' around 'til he comes up with the readies."

"Brilliant!" cried Marietta. "I'll go!"

Everyone looked at her, bemused.

"Er – no, darlin'," said Ma, at length. "That ain't a good idea."

"But I know the way!" argued Marietta. "Oh, let me, please! I've always wanted to hurl a rock through the study window. I'd come straight back, really. You can send somebody with me. I can point out the hole in the tree and everything. And I know a really good place to hide!"

"No. It wouldn't be right."

"But I want to help!" pleaded Marietta. "This is my first ever kidnapping. I want to be *involved*!"

"Ya *are* involved, honey," pointed out Ma, soothingly. "But we cain't have ya deliverin' yer own ransom note. Ratsy an' Burk'll go. You can help by givin' directions."

Marietta looked mutinous and kicked at a stone with her foot.

"It's too complicated," she said. "I'll have to draw a map."

There was an uneasy little silence.

"We can't read a map," admitted Ratsy, eventually.

"Well, there's an easy answer to that," said Ma. "Take Nev."

Nev sighed. Things were going from bad to worse.

CHAPTER 5

COURGETTE TOWERS

Ratsy, Burk and Nev sat astride their horses on a dark hilltop and stared down on Courgette Towers. Well, Ratsy and Burk were on horses. Nev was on Venetia. He didn't like the look of the wild bandit steeds and had insisted. Being the only one who could read had its advantages.

It felt good, having the upper hand for once. It felt good being astride Venetia again too, even though she kept trying to nip him.

"Now, that's what I call a *pile*," said Ratsy, in awestruck tones. "Impressive, eh?"

It was, too. Even in the half-light, it was very clear that Courgette Towers was a house of some importance. It was a huge, gabled mansion surrounded by towering stone walls. Massive gates, rolling lawns, sweeping driveway, well-stocked flower beds, marble statuary, lake, summer house, stables, coach house – it had the lot.

"We'd better ride down and circle round to the back," said Nev, consulting the map.

It was a very good map. Not only had Marietta carefully marked out the way down the mountain and the most sensible route to take through the maze of country lanes in the valley below, she had helpfully drawn a floor plan of the house itself, marking out the study.

"Why the study?" Nev had asked.

"Because it's round the back. There's a

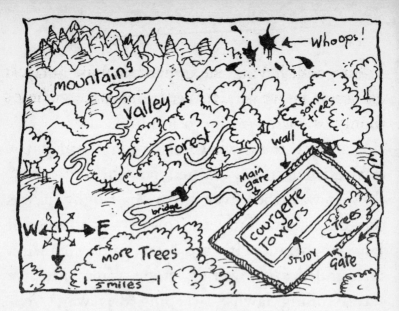

little gate in the wall. Once you're through, there are trees you can hide behind. And it's got the biggest window, so it'll make the loudest crash."

Despite the map, it had taken them a long, long time to cover the distance between the cave and Courgette Towers. It was now dusk and the air was cool.

"Where's the old bridge, then, Nev?" enquired Ratsy.

"There," said Nev, squinting down at the map then pointing to a clump of trees that lay a few hundred yards outside the wall. "See where the river goes into the trees? That's where the hollow oak is. And that's where we make for, just as soon as we've delivered the note. There's plenty of cover."

"Best leave the horses here and go on down by foot," said Ratsy. "And no noise from now on. Right, Burk?"

"URURURUR..."

"Burk!"

"UR? OH. Ururur."

Stiffly, the three of them dismounted, tethered their steeds and set off down the hill. It took longer than they thought. By the time they had skirted the wall of the estate and reached the small gate, dusk had merged into serious night-time. Luckily, there was a moon.

"It's barred!" hissed Nev, pushing in vain. "What shall we do?"

Burk's massive arm reached out and swept him to one side. He placed both palms on the wood and applied slight pressure. There was a squealing, tearing noise, then the hinges gave way and the gate fell away from them, landing with a soft plop on the grass beyond.

There were trees inside, just as Marietta had said there would be. They dodged between them, keeping low to the ground, Ratsy in the lead, followed by Nev, then Burk. Small furry creatures skittered away at their approaching feet. A bird launched itself from a branch with a startled shriek.

"What's happening?" Nev whispered into the darkness. "Where's the house? We must be nearly there now! Ratsy, where are you? I can't see a – ooof!"

He collided painfully with Ratsy, who had come to a crouching halt.

"Ssssh!" hissed Ratsy. "Look." Silently, he pointed.

Nev looked. The trees had thinned out. They were standing a mere few yards away from a large window. Unexpectedly, the room beyond was filled with light. A chandelier, lit with a hundred candles, hung from the high ceiling, shedding its light on the leather-bound books that lined the walls. Even worse, the room was

occupied! A thin, gaunt-faced man in a red velvet jacket was sitting in a leather armchair. A monocle was screwed into one eye. He was reading a book and sipping from a glass of red wine. If he should chance to glance up, he would be looking directly at them!

With one accord, they dived back under cover of the trees.

"Now what?" hissed Nev. His heart was hammering and he felt sick. "She didn't say it would be occupied! That must be her uncle in there! This wasn't supposed to happen. What do we do?"

"Chuck the rock through the window, like we said," said Ratsy. "What difference does it make? Just means he'll get the note sooner. Got the rock, Burk?"

"But you can't go throwing a rock through the window with him sitting there. He might get hit! There'll be broken glass everywhere! Think of the carpet!"

"Nev," said Ratsy. "Just stick to the reading an' writing side of things and leave the action to us, all right? Ready, Burk?"

"No! I forbid it! You can't—"

CRASH! The world exploded in shards of glass.

Nev just had time to see Lord Courgette leap to his feet, spilling his wine in the process, before Burk's paw firmly grasped the collar of his 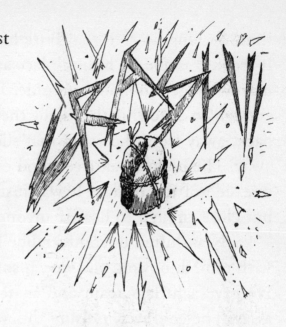 jerkin and he found himself being propelled at top speed back through the trees. Seconds later, they were through the opening in the wall and running across open ground towards the river

---

"Irresponsible, that's what you are!" hissed Nev. His voice echoed unpleasantly. "Irresponsible and – and lacking in responsibility."

"So?" argued Ratsy. "We're bandits. Where does it say bandits 'ave to be responsible?"

It was dark under the bridge. Dark, dank and drippy. They had been sitting there for some time. So long, in fact, that Burk had nodded off. It seemed as good a hiding-place as anywhere. A narrow ledge ran along one side. It was just big enough to sit on, if they kept their feet tucked back, away from the water that slid past, inches away. The hollow oak tree stood on the bank to one side of the bridge. It was just out of sight, but close enough to hear if anyone approached.

Nev shifted uncomfortably. His hand met with something cold and wet. It sort of – pulsed. He gave a little scream and snatched his hand away. The cold wet, pulsing thing gave a croak and jumped into the river.

"Sssssh!" hissed Ratsy.

"But I just put my hand on a *frog*…"

"Just pipe down, will yer? It's all part o' the bandit experience. It ain't all fun an' games. Bandits has to learn to lie low fer long periods o' time. Else yer gives away yer position."

"I want to give away my position," snapped Nev. "I want to give it to *you*. You might not have noticed, but my bit of ledge is narrower than yours. I'm bent double with my chin on my knees and a brick sticking in my back. How much longer must we sit here, anyway? What on earth is Lord Courgette doing? It's been ages since he got the note."

"Patience, son. 'E'll be countin' out the dosh, won't he? Takes a while ter count out eight hundred coins. An' he'll keep getting' it wrong, I shouldn't wonder. I mean, 'e'll be in a bit of a tiz, won't 'e? All upset an' worried. Stands to reason, wiv 'is beloved niece bein' 'eld 'ostage. 'E'll 'ave ter keep stoppin' ter tear 'is 'air out an' 'ave a little weep."

"Hm," said Nev, doubtfully, thinking of the man in the study calmly sipping wine and reading his book. "He didn't look all that worried to me. There weren't any chunks of torn-out hair on the carpet as far as I could see. Plenty of *glass*, mind."

"True. But then, 'e's a lord, ain't 'e? A haristocrat. Stiff upper lip an' that. They're trained to keep their feelings under control, ain't they?"

"You can't have it both ways," argued Nev. "Either he's tearing his hair out and weeping or he's keeping his lip stiff. He'd have to be a contortionist to do both."

"You do go on, don't you, young Nev?" said Ratsy, sounding a little tired. "Why don't you just relax? It's worth puttin' up with a bit of inconvenience fer eight 'undred gold coins"

"What will you do with your share?" asked Nev. There was a little pause. Burk, on the far side of Ratsy, was snoring gently.

"Tell you somethin', kid," said Ratsy, confidentially. "Lately, I bin dreamin' of a little farm. Not too big. Just a coupla acres. A cow, a goat, a few chickens runnin' around the yard. Plump little wife wiv apple cheeks, wearin' one o' them dresses wiv the little squares, you know?

An' kids. Three of 'em. Johnny, Clara an' little Sidney."

"Really?" said Nev. "Well, well. You do surprise me, Ratsy. I would never have guessed you would spend your money on a farm."

"Eh? Who said anythin' about spendin' me money on a farm?"

"Why – *you* did."

"No I never. I said I bin *dreamin'* about a farm. Burk's snorin' reminded me, that's all. Oh no – I'm gonna spend me money down the pub, same as I always do. I was just passin' the time, tellin' about me dream. The other night I 'ad one about a jellyfish an' a teapot. I lifts the lid o' this teapot, yer see, an'..."

He broke off abruptly. Above them, a twig crackled.

Ratsy dug Burk in the ribs, and his snores ceased instantly. The three of them froze. Somebody was up there all right. They could hear footsteps rustling in the fallen leaves. There came the sound of a muffled cough, followed by a curious tapping noise. Moments later, the tapping stopped and the footsteps receded briskly into the distance.

The three hidden beneath the bridge waited for a few minutes, just to make sure. Then:

"We've done it!" crowed Ratsy. "Come on, lads! Let's go and collect the dosh! Out you go, Nev, what you waitin' for?" He gave him a push.

"All right, all right, I'm going," said Nev.

He unfolded his cramped legs and crawled along the ledge, feeling carefully for any more stray frogs. When he reached the end, he cautiously poked his head out. Everything was still. At the top of the bank stood the oak tree, the full moon caught in its spreading branches.

"All clear?" came Ratsy's voice from behind him.

"Yes, I think so."

"Then let's go!"

Slipping and sliding, they climbed up the muddy bank. Eagerly, they approached the oak tree. There was a large hole in the trunk, just as Marietta had described. It was just the right size to take a bulging bag full of coins.

Sadly, the hole remained empty. Nailed to

the trunk, just above the hole, however, was a small piece of paper.

"What's it say, Nev?" asked Ratsy.

"You're not going to like this," said Nev, staring in disbelief.

The note consisted of a single crisp, short word. It read:

CHAPTER 6
ESCAPE

"It said *what*?" gasped Ma, in disbelief.

"*NO*," said Neville, for the third time. "That's all it said. *NO*."

"You sure you read it right?"

"Of course I did. You can't go wrong with *NO*. The hole was empty and the note said *NO*. So that's it. No ransom. "

"After all we went through," said Ratsy,

miserably. "All that ridin' an' sneakin' about an' hidin' under drippy bridges an' everythin'."

"Seems unbelievable!" cried Ma. "His only niece in the hands of thieves an' cut-throats and he's refusin' ter pay up? Whatever kind of a monster is he?"

All eyes turned to Marietta. She was sitting quietly by herself, stroking Spot. By her side lay a pile of silky squares. She had been whiling away the time cutting up her dresses into cushion covers. She looked up and gave a tired little shrug.

"Sorry," she said. Then she stood up and walked out of the cave. Spot gave a sympathetic whimper, looked as though he might follow her, then noticed that there was still a bit of stew left in the unattended cooking pot and changed his mind.

Nobody said anything. Disappointment hung in the air like fog. In silence, the bandits retreated to their various mattresses, lay down and covered themselves with bits of sack. Still shaking her head, Ma retired to her hammock. She didn't even order anybody to take the watch. It was clear that there was to be no card games, singing or shooting at bottles that night. It was as though the stuffing had been knocked out of everybody.

Nev walked out of the cave. Nobody asked him where he was going.

Outside, the moon still hung in the sky. Marietta was sitting on the rock, gazing into the trees. He walked over to her and sat down.

"What's wrong?" he asked, after a bit.

"Uncle," muttered Marietta. "He's what's wrong."

"I don't understand," said Nev. She turned to him, eyes flashing.

"Isn't it obvious? He hates me. Ever since Father and Mother left, he's tried to get rid of me. He keeps sending me off to horrible boarding schools. I hate them. I can't count how many times I've run away."

"Your parents – left?"

"Father had to go away overseas on business and Mother went with him. Uncle promised to take care of me. They gave him lots of money to pay for my keep. They were supposed to come back in six months. That was seven years ago."

"*Seven years*? But – didn't they write, or anything?"

"Not a word."

"But – didn't your uncle make enquiries?"

"According to him, the ship they sailed on never docked. He says they're – they're…" She couldn't finish the sentence. Nev fished in his jerkin and found a reasonably clean rag.

"Here," he said, gently. "Use this."

They sat quietly for a moment while Marietta blew her nose. Spot appeared from the cave mouth, trotted over and laid his head on her lap. She tugged his ears, gave a little sigh, then suddenly stood up.

"That's enough of that," she said. "Come on."

"What?" said Nev, startled. "Where?"

"To Courgette Towers. We're leaving."

"But I thought you said that was the last place you wanted to be. I thought you said…"

"Never mind what I said. The adventure's over – for me, at any rate. I'm no use to Ma and the bandits now. But at least I can do something for you. Is there anything you need from the cave?"

"Venetia's saddle. And my axe and my spare socks. But…"

"Go and get them, then. They'll all be asleep by now. It's the perfect time. What's the matter? Don't you want to escape?"

"Well, yes, of course, but…"

"Hurry up, then. I'll fetch Venetia."

Briskly, she turned and walked to where the horses were grazing. Nev stood. Spot shot to his feet, tail wagging.

"Stay," Nev told him. "And keep quiet. I'll be right back." Then, for the last time, he entered the cave.

The snoring was so thick, you could cut it with a knife. Nobody stirred as he tiptoed over to the pile of saddles and removed the smallest, oldest one, which was Venetia's. Hardly daring to breathe, he crept over to his mattress, fumbled beneath and drew out his axe and the spotted bundle containing his precious spare socks.

He cast his eyes over the tattered, slumbering bodies that littered the cave. Would he miss them? Well, yes, in some ways, he would. They hadn't treated him too badly, all things considered. But the time had come to move on. One hundred gold coins. That was what mattered.

Ten minutes later, he and Marietta were squashed together on Venetia's back, with Spot running merrily at her heels, on their way back down the mountain to Courgette Towers.

CHAPTER 7

THE REWARD

"Miss Marietta! Can it be? You've come back to us! Oh, may the heavens be praised!"

The old man standing on the doorstep broke into a delighted grin.

"Good morning, Trimble. Is my uncle up?"

"Oh, yes, miss. He's in the breakfast room, waiting for the men to come and fix the study window. It got smashed last night, you know, terrible business…"

"I know. Look, we'll just go straight on in and see him. No need to announce us. Come on, Nev."

Briskly, she marched past.

"Er – right," said Nev. "Spot, stay there. I won't be long."

With an apologetic little smile, he sidled past the butler and followed Marietta across the enormous entrance hall and down a long, thickly-carpeted corridor, hung with oil paintings. He caught up with her just as she stopped by a tall, carved door.

"I'll do the talking, all right?"

she said. "You rescued me. That's all you need to know."

"But I didn't. You just walked out and I came with you…"

"Oh, please! Stop being so annoyingly *honest* for once. Just back me up." And with that, she wrenched it open.

Lord Courgette was sitting at an elegant table. Before him was a silver coffee pot, milk jug and china cup and saucer. He looked up as Marietta and Neville entered the room. His face was expressionless.

"Well, well," he said, after a little pause.

"There you are, Marietta. I was wondering how long it would take before you tired of your latest little escapade. And here you are, safe and sound."

"No thanks to you!" snapped Marietta.

"Oh, come, come, my dear. Surely you didn't expect me to respond to that ludicrous little note? I knew you would be back when it suited you. You always turn up eventually. Like the proverbial bad penny."

Nev could hardly believe his ears. He had heard of wicked uncles in fairy tales, but this one took the cake. Calmly, Lord Courgette poured himself a cup of coffee. He leaned back in his chair and sipped it.

"So tell me, Marietta. Who is this young fellow currently spreading mud all over my carpet?"

"This is a friend of mine," Marietta told him, coldly. "You've him to thank for rescuing me."

"Indeed?" said Lord Courgette, raising one eyebrow. "Well, young man, that's all very fine and noble, but I hardly think you need have gone to any trouble. My niece here is quite capable of escaping all on her own, isn't that right, my dear? How many boarding schools have you run away from, Marietta? Six, is it? Or seven? I quite lose count."

"Excuse me, sir," said Nev, stiffly. Marietta had told him to let her do the talking, but he just couldn't help it. "I think this occasion was rather different, if you don't mind my saying so. It's hardly the same as boarding school, is it? Being held for ransom by a vicious gang of cutthroats and thieves…"

"Yes, yes, nanny told me all about it," interrupted his lordship, impatiently.

"Well, then, surely…"

"Surely nothing! You know nothing of my niece, young man. It may surprise you to learn that beneath that innocent face lies a scheming young minx who's only purpose in life is to cause me trouble. Isn't that right, Marietta?"

"Maybe," agreed Marietta. Her face was red with fury. "But, that's got nothing to do with Nev. It was him that rescued me and the least you can do is reward him for his trouble."

"Reward?" Lord Courgette's lip curled. "Reward, did you say?"

"Yes!" Marietta stamped her foot. "I promised him! I promised!"

"And how much *reward* did you promise this – this grubby bandit boy?"

"One hundred gold coins. That's what he

needs to go straight."

There was a little pause. Then, Lord Courgette began to laugh. There was no humour in the sound. He threw back his head and roared, while Nev looked on, speechless. Suddenly, he stopped, dabbed his mouth with a napkin and rose to his feet. "Ridiculous!" he snapped. "I'll hear no more of this. Get out of my house, boy, before I have you thrown out. Marietta, go to your room. I shall speak to you later. There's a little matter of a sapphire bracelet and some diamond rings you helped yourself to."

"They weren't yours! They belonged to Mother!"

"I'm not arguing with you, girl. Get to your room."

Marietta stood her ground.

"One hundred gold coins," she repeated steadily. "That's what he needs to be on his way. But if you don't give it to him, he won't have any option but to resume his life of crime. He'll return to the bandits, won't you, Nev? And, believe me, they're pretty fed up with you already. One word from him, and every night

95

from now on, you can expect a rock through the study window. Or maybe a fire in the coach house. And you'll need to employ extra staff to guard the stables, because I have a feeling a few horses might go missing. Isn't that right, Nev? Tell him."

"Oh – er – yes," agreed Nev. "We're – em – pretty tough when we're crossed."

"You wouldn't dare," hissed his lordship. "Blackmail me? You wouldn't *dare*!"

"Oh no?" said Nev. He looked Lord Courgette straight in the eye. "Try me."

Many hours later, beneath a sky sprinkled thickly with stars, Nev lay sleeping by the side of the road. A short way along, the road forked. A two-pronged signpost stood at the division. One sign read *To the Sea* and the other said *To the Forest*. Venetia was dozing on her feet beneath a clump of nearby trees. Spot was spread across his feet, like a furry blanket.

Beneath his head was a bulging sack containing *one hundred gold coins!*

(POSTSCRIPT)

Nev was dreaming. In his dream, he was standing on the top step of Courgette Towers. Lord Courgette was shouting at him, ordering him off the property. In the shadowy hallway he caught a glimpse of Marietta's face. It was white, but triumphant.

"Good luck, Nev!" she was shouting. "Take care!"

"But what about you?"

"I'll be fine! Whatever happens, don't..."

But he never learnt what she was about to say, because the great door slammed shut in his face.

Nev whimpered and stirred in his sleep. Lying next to him was a picture postcard. It showed a lovely view of the mountains. He had bought it from a little shop in one of the villages he had passed through earlier that day. He hadn't wanted to dip into the sack of gold coins, but the kindly old lady who ran the shop had let him have the postcard in exchange for him chopping up some kindling. Of course, it would probably arrive home after him – but he would post it anyway. It said:

DErE GraN,
Grate NOOs. I hav
goT ThE munny.
I am on my WAY hom.
. I wil bE with you
iN a day or Too.
Dunt wurry.
YoRE LOViNk grandsun
Nev. X

Gran
PlumtrEE
Cottage
FinglE FoRESt.

AFFIX
STAMP
HERE.

So, reader. Does he make it? Find out in the next *gripping* instalment…

Another Hodder Children's Book

THE QUEST FOR 100 GOLD COINS

Kaye Umansky

Illustrated by: Chris Fisher

Part One:
Donkey-ride to Disaster

Poor old Nev Niceguy. His job as a humble
woodcutter barely puts food on the table –
and now he and his dotty old gran owe
YEARS of backrent! If they can't find the
money, they're out in the forest . . .
What's a niceguy to do?

Armed with sandwiches and his trusty axe
Nev prepares to go it alone; to seek out and
bring home one hundred gold coins. But will
he survive the big wide world?

Hold on to your seat – it's the adventure of a lifetime!

THE QUEST FOR 100 GOLD COINS

Kaye Umansky

Illustrated by: Chris Fisher

Part Three:
Strange Days at Sea

Poor old Nev Niceguy. His job as a humble woodcutter barely puts food on the table – and now he and his dotty old gran owe YEARS of backrent! If they can't find the money, they're out in the forest . . . What's a niceguy to do?

Desperate for cash, poor old Nev heads for the sea, and before he knows it he's setting sail on *The Dandy's Revenge*. Surrounded by nutters – and all the cabbage he can eat – Nev is beginning to feel a teeny bit unlucky. Will he ever see home again . . ?

Hold on to your seats – its the adventure of a lifetime!

THE QUEST FOR 100 GOLD COINS

Kaye Umansky

Illustrated by: Chris Fisher

Part Four:
No More Master Niceguy

Poor old Nev Niceguy. His job as a humble
woodcutter barely puts food on the table – and
now he and his dotty old gran owe YEARS of
backrent! If they can't find the money, they're out in
the forest . . . What's a niceguy to do?

Nev has done it! He's got the money and now he
can't wait to see the look on dear old Gran's face.
But someone should have warned Nev about talking
to strangers – especially if they've got a hooked nose
and a rather wicked cackle . . .

Hold on to your seats – it's the adventure of a lifetime!

HAMMY HOUSE OF HORROR

Kaye Umansky

Illustrated by: Chris Fisher

A wild wintry night. An icy wind. A mighty castle.

As Professor Von Strudel (a very brainy guinea pig) and his faithful assistant, Hamish (a not so brainy hamster), make their way to the castle of Count Ratula, they have no idea what's in store. Greeted by a roaring fire, and a banquet fit for royalty, perhaps their stay will be something special? Or perhaps they should have listened to their friends' warnings? After all, Fritz the hedgehog and Gretchen the mouse have lived under the dark shadow of this particular castle for longer than most . . .

Another Hodder Children's Book

BEYOND THE BEANSTALK

Kaye Umansky

Illustrated by: Chris Fisher

The hilarious sequel to *Jack and the Beanstalk* . . .

Jack the Giant Killer finds being rich a lonely
business. And when the final golden egg is
gone, there's nothing for it but to sell the
palace and move back to a humble cottage.

Only his mother is not happy. And Jack is
no longer a hero.

When old Mother Skinnard hands him three magic
beans, how can he possibly resist? And when they
grow into a magnificent beanstalk in the middle
of the night, what choice does he have but to climb
back up to the land of the giants?